BAD BEARS in the BIG CITY

An **IRVING** & **MUKTUK** Story

DANIEL PINKWATER
Illustrated by **JILL PINKWATER**

Houghton Mifflin
Boston

For Larry.
Where are you???

Text copyright © 2003 by Daniel Pinkwater
Illustrations copyright © 2003 by Jill Pinkwater

www.houghtonmifflinbooks.com

The text of this book is set in 12-point Leawood.
The illustrations were created with
felt-tip marker and ink on Bristol board.

Library of Congress Cataloging-in-Publication Data
Pinkwater, Daniel Manus, 1941–
Bad Bears in the big city: An Irving and Muktuk story / Daniel Pinkwater;
illustrated by Jill Pinkwater.
p. cm.
Summary: Irving and Muktuk, two muffin-eating polar bears from the frozen north,
have some trouble fitting into life at the zoo in Bayonne, New Jersey.
HC ISBN 0-618-25208-8   PA ISBN 0-618-68952-4
[1. Polar bear—Fiction. 2. Bears—Fiction. 3. Zoos—Fiction.
4. Humorous stories.] I. Pinkwater, Jill, ill. II. Title.
PZ7.P6335 Bad 2003
[E]—dc21   2002151192

HC ISBN-13: 978-0618-25208-4
PA ISBN-13: 978-0618-68952-1

Printed in Singapore
TWP 10 9 8 7 6 5 4 3 2

It is the midnight flight from Yellowtooth in the far frozen North. Tonight the airplane brings something special — two polar bears for the Bayonne, New Jersey, Zoo.

The Director of the Zoo and the Head Zookeeper wait near the cargo door at the rear of the aircraft.

"The bears will be in a large cage or perhaps a box," the Head Zookeeper tells the Zoo Director. He does not see Irving and Muktuk come down the stairs with the other passengers.

Irving has an envelope. He gives it to the Zoo Director. It is a letter from Officer Bunny. Officer Bunny represents the law in Yellowtooth. He writes, "We hope you enjoy our bears. Remember, they are not to be trusted!"

The Director of the Zoo and the Head Zookeeper escort Irving and Muktuk to the zoo bus, and they are driven to their new home. Next to the zoo is a large muffin factory.

At the zoo, the Bear Keeper, Mr. Goldberg, shows them their lockers. "Here are your pillows. After you have slept, you may put them in your lockers. Tomorrow you will meet Roy. Roy is the other polar bear."

In the morning they meet Roy.
Roy says, "I heard you were kicked out
of Yellowtooth for stealing muffins."

"We were kicked out of Yellowtooth
for stealing *lots* of muffins," Muktuk says.
Irving drools.
"That building is a muffin factory,
is it not?" Muktuk asks.
"It is," Roy says.

"It is right beside the zoo,"
says Irving.
"Yes, it is," says Roy.

"Where were you last night?" Muktuk asks Roy.

"I was home," says Roy.

"Home?" Irving asks. "You don't sleep in the zoo?"

"I have an apartment," says Roy.

"And that is like . . . ?" Muktuk asks.

"Rooms that are just for me," Roy says. "I have a freezer. I have four air conditioners. I have two electric fans."

"What's in the freezer?" Irving asks.

"What do you think?" Roy asks.

"Muffins?"

"I have fish cakes, too," Roy says.

"Can we have an apartment?" Irving asks.

"I don't think so," Roy says.

"Why not?"

"You're not to be trusted."

"Because they are afraid we might break in to the muffin factory?"

"Because they are afraid you might eat people."

"You can eat people?"

"Don't even think about it."

"It is time to go to work," Roy says.

"Work? We have to work?" Irving and Muktuk ask.

"Sure," Roy says. "It is easy. Do what I do."

Irving and Muktuk follow Roy through a door to the polar bear area. There is a waterfall. There is a pool. There are rocks.

"This is nice," Muktuk says.

"I'm taking a swim," Irving says.

"Wave to the people," Roy says.

All day Irving, Muktuk, and Roy dive and swim. They wave to people who visit the zoo. The people throw them muffins and sometimes fish. The bears climb on the rocks and take naps.

Twice, Mr. Goldberg, the Bear Keeper, comes with food.

"What is this stuff?" Irving and Muktuk ask.

"Bear chow," says Roy. "Not bad, huh?"

"It's okay," say Irving and Muktuk. "Muffins would be better."

At six o'clock the zoo is closed. No more visitors are allowed in.

"It was nice working with you," says Roy. "I'll see you tomorrow."

"Can't we come with you?" Irving and Muktuk ask.

"They won't allow it. You're not to be trusted."

"You know, we've never eaten a person," Muktuk says. "In Yellowtooth maybe we took a few muffins. That's all."

Roy goes to his locker. He puts on his hat. He puts on his coat, swipes his timecard through the slot under the big clock, and goes to wait for the bus.

Irving and Muktuk spend the evening playing with an old deck of cards and making plans for breaking in to the muffin factory.

Even though they have been thrown muffins, Irving and Muktuk dream of having more.

For the rest of the week, Irving, Muktuk, and Roy continue to entertain zoo visitors. Mr. Goldberg gives them a large ball, and they have fun inventing games. Every night Roy goes home on the bus and Irving and Muktuk pass the time as best they can.

The zoo is closed on Monday. Irving and Muktuk become bored and restless.

"Where is Roy?" asks Irving.

"Let's go and find him," says Muktuk.

They put their pillows on their heads, drape blankets over their shoulders, swipe the three of diamonds and the five of clubs through the slot under the big clock, and leave the zoo.

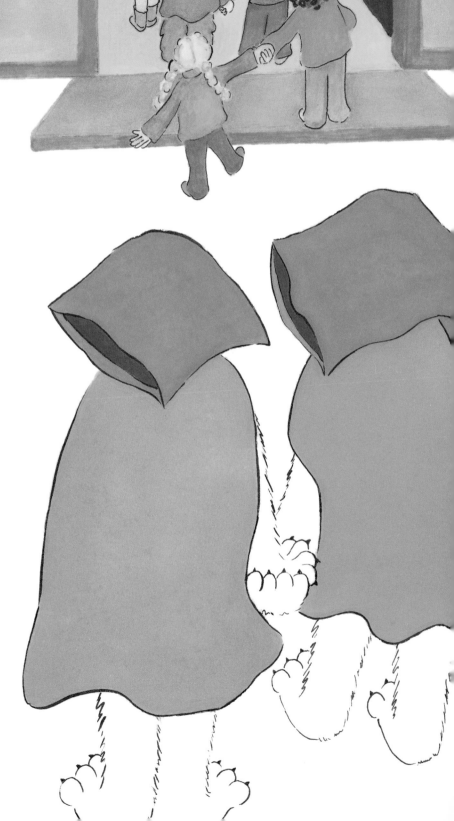

Outside the zoo, Irving and Muktuk join a line behind some children. It is the nine o'clock tour of the muffin factory, just about to begin.

The children's teacher says, "Stay close together, hold hands, and do not talk. Now, follow me into the muffin factory. We will learn many interesting things."

Irving and Muktuk stand close together. They hold hands. They follow the children into the muffin factory.

They learn many interesting things. At the end of the tour the children and their teacher and Irving and Muktuk are invited to eat all the muffins they want. It is at this point that Irving and Muktuk are discovered to be bears.

Before the zookeepers can arrive, Irving and Muktuk leave the muffin factory and go in search of Roy. They do not find him, but Roy finds them. Roy finds them lying down in the frozen food section of a large supermarket.

"What are you doing?" asks Roy. "The police have been sent for."

"We became warm and tired," Irving and Muktuk say. "We are lying on frozen peas. Is your apartment nearby?"

Roy telephones the Head Zookeeper.

"They are here, in my apartment," Roy says. "I found them in the supermarket. They were lying on frozen peas."

The Head Zookeeper tells Roy to keep Irving and Muktuk with him. The Zoo Director, the Head Zookeeper, and Mr. Goldberg will be right there.

"You're in trouble now," Roy tells Irving and Muktuk.

Irving and Muktuk begin to cry.

"Oh, please!" Irving and Muktuk say. "We don't want to be in trouble! Tell the Zoo Director, the Head Zookeeper, and Mr. Goldberg that we are to be trusted!"

"Are you to be trusted? Really?" Roy asks.

"Well, about what you said . . . about eating people. We are to be trusted about that," Irving and Muktuk say.

The Zoo Director, the Head Zookeeper,
and Mr. Goldberg arrive.

"They left the zoo without permission," the Zoo Director says.
"They are not to be trusted," the Head Zookeeper says.
"They are bad bears," Mr. Goldberg says.

"They are bad bears, I have to say it," Roy says. "But they have assured me they will not eat people."

"Is this true?" the Zoo Director, the Head Zookeeper, and Mr. Goldberg ask Irving and Muktuk.

Irving and Muktuk are still crying. They blow their noses and nod their heads.

"Perhaps on Mondays, when the zoo is closed, they could stay with me," Roy says. "After a while, if they have not eaten any people, the zoo can give them more freedom."

"What about things like entering the muffin factory, and lying on frozen peas?" the Zoo Director asks. "Can you discourage them?"
"I will do my best," Roy says.